THE DOG STAYS

AND OTHER STORIES

THE DOG STAYS

AND OTHER STORIES

MARJAN SIERHUIS

IGUANA

Copyright © 2023 Marjan Sierhuis
Published by Iguana Books
720 Bathurst Street, Suite 410
Toronto, ON M5S 2R4

Publisher: Cheryl Hawley
Editor: Paula Chiarcos
Front cover design: Ruth Dwight, designplayground.ca

ISBN 978-1-77180-613-8 (paperback)

This is an original print edition of *The Dog Stays and Other Stories*.

For my nephew, Greg

A Blue Baby Hat

Outside the window, clouds drift across the night sky and offer white dreams to those who sleep. But they appear to have forgotten James. His eyes are closed but he's aware of the cacophony of sounds. They creep stealthily through the cracks in the door and intrude upon his privacy within.

His tired eyes are filled with unshed tears as he stretches his arm across white hospital sheets. He tenderly covers his wife's cold hand with his. He waits for a sign. Fluttering movements from long eyelashes that brush her pale cheeks or a tongue that teases dry lips.

James tries not to focus on a mechanical ventilator that sits idle in a corner of the room. He ignores the nasal cannula that drapes over and behind his wife's delicate ears.

His eyes drift to her chest, rising and falling with every breath.

Carefully, he pulls a blue baby hat out of his trouser pocket. He lays the brand-new knit by the corner of his wife's pillow.

He leans over and gently places his unshaven face against her soft skin.

A tear rolls down her cheek, caressing the side of her face.

He takes a deep breath, savours the moment, and knows that everything will be all right.

Flame

Flame is deep in thought this morning as she stands by a river that flows behind the film set. Often a voracious eater, a pile of uneaten fish lies by her feet.

"Gentleheart, you are a dragon. The world can be a dangerous place for those who are different," said her mother years ago when Flame told her of her plans to leave home.

"I want to prove I can live on my own," said Flame and bowed her head.

Her mother worried for her youngest child but offered Flame her blessing and told her she was always welcome home.

Cedric, a director of fantasy films, feels his heart pounding in his chest as he approaches Flame. He is troubled by dragons. This one is no exception. Perspiration dampens his forehead and trickles into the folds of his neck. Maintaining a respectable distance, he waits for his presence to be acknowledged.

Flame looks up and recognizes Cedric. The sour look on his face makes her take a deep breath.

"I need to talk to you," he says with arms crossed.

Flame musters up enough courage to move closer. She peeks out the corner of a yellow eye and nearly sweeps him off his feet as she spreads her bat-like wings.

Cedric refuses to be intimidated. "The producers want to use CGI instead of ... of you," Cedric says.

The studio must have forgotten their promise. *You could be a major star someday. We'll do our best to see you get there.*

Cedric takes a deep breath and moves forward. "Sorry about this, but budget constraints, you know? And a bunch of our film sets have disappeared in a ... a puff of smoke." He pauses. "And our water bills are enormous, and insurance premiums — don't even get me started."

Flame shakes her head. Here she is, a film extra with no benefits or pension plan. She does what she's told, without asking questions. She accepts a pittance of a salary after working long hours.

"Sorry," says Cedric. "We have no choice."

"No, no, no!" Flame screams.

"You're fired. There's nothing more I have to say about the matter." Cedric turns away.

Flame puffs out her chest. She flicks her tongue, flares her nostrils, and encircles Cedric's body with her scaly tail. Drawing on elemental energy that courses through her veins, she gives a low growl as she takes flight.

"Ouch! Put me down so we can talk about it!" yells Cedric.

Later, in the dragon's lair, Flame unfurls her tail and releases her unsteady passenger.

"I'm sorry but I had no choice," she says as she watches Cedric crawl behind a nearby boulder. "You have no idea how hard it is to be a film extra. When I breathe fire, it depletes all my energy. I could have auditioned for a speaking part, like the other dragons, but they kept telling me I needed to work on my enunciation."

Cedric sees the dragon in a new light. He leaves the security of the rock and approaches Flame.

Flame speaks in a softer tone. She promises never to repeat such foolish behaviour.

Cedric vows to attend a workshop on communication.

They discuss Flame's future in the movie industry and how she can achieve her goals. And after a tour of the lair, Cedric leaves on his own.

Months later, Cedric throws fish to Flame while he helps his friend rehearse her lines.

Please Stay

Barbara sits by her husband's bedside and glances at their wedding photo on the nightstand.

She strokes his damp cheek with the tip of her finger, kisses his forehead, and holds on to his cold hand. She's afraid to let go. The thought of his impending death makes her shiver. She wonders how she will cope without him.

She prays that he says a few final words. She would love to hear his voice one last time.

Barbara is not greedy. One or two words will do. She has learned to lower her expectations.

While his eyes remain closed, hers fill with unshed tears as she commits every feature to memory.

"You're still a handsome man, Carter," she says out loud.

She snuggles up beside him in bed, just like old times, and whispers in his ear.

Although he may still hear her voice, she fears he may no longer recognize it.

After all, his memories were taken long ago.

Gobble

Butch is anxious this morning. His goose is cooked if he receives no reprieve. The ground-dwelling bird waits anxiously as the farmer approaches his enclosed area.

From a distance, the farmer's wife, in her waterproof boots, cries out, "We need to talk!"

But Joshua knows what his wife wants to say. After all, it is the same old, same old thing every Thanksgiving.

"The subject is closed," he says.

In the meantime, Butch struts around. He utters gobbling sounds and then perches on a bale of straw. With some trepidation, he watches the gate open.

Face flushed, Joshua's wife reaches her husband and waves a sheet of paper in his face.

"Butch is granted a pardon this year."

Joshua shrugs. His wife's pet turkey gets to live another day.

Fowl Mood

Brian enters the walk-in clinic in distress and informs the receptionist he needs to see a doctor at once.

"I'm feeling unwell." He sniffles and blows his nose. "My allergies are bothering me."

"Health card, please. Any changes in address or phone number? Okay, take a seat in the waiting room. The doctor will be with you shortly."

Brian enters the waiting area and sits on the only available chair. Then stands up and returns to the desk.

The receptionist eyes him. "Sir, may I help you?"

"The only available chair is beside a turkey who is giving his owner a hard time. I think I'll come back tomorrow."

Potty Mouth

She stops by the home office and watches her husband tap on his keyboard.

"Charlie is being unusually quiet," says Richard.

"The last time I looked in on him, he was hanging upside down in his cage, purring," says Michelle.

From the living room, a hissing sound is followed by a low growl.

Richard looks up. "Oh my, that doesn't sound good."

Minutes later, the family cat slinks into the office and crawls beneath the desk. Grey feathers hang out of her mouth.

Michelle dashes into the living room. She speaks softly to her frustrated bird who is now cursing up a storm. She'll teach Charlie some new words when he's in a better frame of mind.

Thumper

Thumper, with a fluffy white tail and upright ears, bounces gleefully through the park. It's a beautiful spring day. Overhead, a clear blue sky extends for miles.

A child's laughter breaks the silence. Egad, it's that time of year again.

Voices draw near.

Thumper hides behind an oak tree — shelter until he decides what to do.

A young boy appears and looks around. "I think I saw him hop in this direction."

"Johnnie, please don't run off like that."

"But, Dad, you promised me a rabbit this year."

"I know — but not one that runs wild in the park."

Thumper breathes a sigh of relief. Being a rabbit during Easter is causing him too much stress.

The Herd Waits

Three hundred and sixty-five days, come rain or shine, you would visit us at the ranch. As soon as you arrived in your vehicles, the herd and I would cross the pasture. We would walk over to the fence to be near you. But where have you been? Have you been sick? We hope not. Our owners never tell us anything. So please come. We miss your laughter and smiles. We'll be waiting.

The Alarm Clock

Aurora unlocked her car door. She placed her purse on the passenger seat. As she drove down the street, she found the neighbourhood unusually quiet.

She wondered if the neighbours had already left for work. But according to her antique wristwatch, it was only 8:00 a.m.

Sixty minutes later, she arrived at her destination, grabbed her bag from the seat and walked in the direction of a shopping mall.

As she entered the shoe store, she looked up at a wall clock that showed 10:00 a.m.

"You're late. I hope you have a good explanation," said her boss.

"The flea market vendor said the alarm clock would automatically adjust to daylight saving time," said Aurora.

"And you believed him of course." The boss raised his eyebrows.

"Absolutely," said Aurora with a flushed face.

Bailey

He stands by the front door while he waits for his owner.

Wyatt smiles. "Here I am." He approaches his pet with a leash and a couple of face masks. One for himself, and the other for the dog.

Bailey considers the dog mask an embarrassment. After all, he still has his pride.

He pauses, growls, and runs down the hall.

Wyatt shouts, "Bailey, please stop! Come back. The mask is for your protection. And we could both use the exercise."

Bailey darts into the kitchen. A visit to the water bowl now tops his list of priorities. The walk and dog mask will have to wait until he's in a better frame of mind.

Buried Treasure

Pepper gazes out of her humble abode in an old oak tree. She found her previous digs unacceptable to her discerning taste. Today, she plans to gather enough acorns, seeds, and berries to see her through the winter months. They predict a cold one this year, she has heard. But prying eyes could hinder her plans by hijacking her bumper crop.

Her bushy grey tail swings gracefully during her descent. Her big black eyes scour the vast woodland while she pauses at the base of the tree. She breathes a sigh of relief. The coast is clear. There is no sign of Dexter, her rival. It is time to gather and hide her cache.

An Itchy Nose

"We'll soon be out of here," says Rudy, his booty in the air while his nose sniffs around the fence post.

"Quit digging by the fence," says Max, who sits on his haunches as he waits nearby.

"You're annoying me," says Rudy.

"But remember the last time," says Max. "Quarantined for fourteen days and no doggy treats for seven."

"How can I forget," says Rudy. "You wouldn't stop whining the entire time, and I didn't get a wink of sleep."

"Be quiet. I hear someone coming."

Charlotte approaches her precious animals. She fits each one with an air-filter face mask, attaches a standard dog leash, and leads them out of the yard for their morning walk.

Before long, an animal howls.

It's Rudy. He has an itchy nose.

Benji

Annie smiles as she opens the back door for her beloved pooch.

"Go potty."

But Benji has other plans, and he wastes no time. He runs to a shaded area in the backyard. He needs to dig lickety-split. Dilly-dallying on his part will draw unwanted attention and interfere with his plans.

He pauses at the foot of an old oak tree. Suddenly anxious, he turns his head. Good. Annie appears preoccupied with a pan on the kitchen stove.

Head down, booty in the air, Benji digs and then digs some more. Finally satisfied, he opens his mouth and lets his favourite stuffed animal drop into the hole.

"Benji, come!"

Quickly he covers the hole.

Thank goodness, he won't have to share his toy with the new puppy.

A Barnyard Meeting

Move closer everyone. Try not to lollygag by the fence.

The meeting will now come to order.

Stock us with hay, grass, and corn, Jack, but try to control your grazing.

Keep a lookout, Petal. Bleat softly if you see someone eavesdrop.

Suppress your enthusiasm, Russell. Your constant crowing gives me a headache and attracts unwanted attention.

Focus on the matter at hand, Frankie. Your squeals can be a major distraction. Although, if you must, try to keep the noise to a minimum.

Get back here, you all. We still need to vote. Should visitors to the farm wear a mask? Stomp once for yes, twice for no.

Tess

Tess scurried on padded paws around an expanse of mighty oak trees that shaded the public park. She crossed mowed grass, oblivious to the gentle fall breeze, which ruffled her glossy grey fur. She headed toward her friend who stood beside one of the park benches.

"Why the hurry?" asked Harlow as he waited for Tess to catch her breath.

Tess flicked her magnificent tail in his direction and exuded too much hip action. Unceremoniously, she knocked him over. But nimble and none the worse for wear, he regained his footing and moved back a few steps.

"Sorry," said Tess as she paused a few minutes and stared at him with her enormous black eyes. "I missed you while you were away." And she proceeded to tell him how her tail had attracted far too much attention from the other squirrels. "They'd come up close and try to touch it without asking my permission."

"So what did you do about it?" asked Harlow in a tone that expressed concern. "I came up with an idea," said Tess. "I told everyone that if they promised to leave my tail alone, I'd still let them hang out with me. But it would be on my terms."

"How is that working out for you?" asked Harlow as he puffed out a breath and teased his palate with an acorn.

Tess grinned. "If you take a nut or two out of the equation, my stockpile now sits at a whopping five thousand, four hundred and twenty-one," she said. "But then who's counting."

Marigold

A beautiful sunny day brings families to a local farm.

Children's voices get louder and louder as the children race along a wooden fence.

Distracted by the noise, Marigold the goat looks up from her lunch. The hay can wait. Her guests are more important.

She glances at her other roommates. Occupied, they appear too busy to socialize and continue to munch.

With hooves flying high, Marigold runs over to the wooden fence. She stares at her visitors and starts to vocalize. She's ready to give them her undivided attention.

Squeals of delight fill the air as little hands reach out to touch her.

Rocky

Rocky was one special rooster. From his barred plumage of black and white to his bright-red comb, wattles, and earlobes, he was an impressive looking cockerel. And lately he learned how to strut his stuff in front of the young ladies.

Feisty and full of energy, he was always vying for the girls' attention. But his interest lay with one hen in particular — although sweet-tempered Daisy wanted nothing to do with the Casanova until he learned to control his crowing.

But that could present a challenge for Rocky. He always had something to say.

The Masked Bandit

Abigail woke to scratching noises coming from her kitchen. She sat up, flipped the switch on her table lamp, and stared at her alarm clock. It read a few minutes past midnight.

As bed sheets slipped from her shoulders, she started to shiver. Had she forgotten to shut the kitchen window before going to bed?

She swore and shook her head as the noise continued. It was time to have a look. She leaped out of bed, crossed the hall, paused outside the entrance to the kitchen, and peeked around the corner. A masked creature was eating from her cat's food bowl while her beloved cat lay cowering beneath the table.

Abigail opened a closet door and grabbed a mop. The masked marauder gave her a blank stare and continued to chew. With the mop held in front of her, Abigail shouted, cursed, and stamped her feet.

Unfazed, the creature grabbed hold of the mop's end with its claws, hissed, snarled, and refused to let go.

Abigail watched in horror as chattering brethren suddenly crawled through the kitchen's open window. They made their way to a box of leftover pizza sitting on the counter and started to eat.

She sighed with relief, hours later when they finally left — or so she thought — until she heard a noise once again coming from the kitchen.

15

The Huntress

The huntress sees her target sitting at a patio table under a cloudless sky. She listens and waits. She wants her initial attack to carry an element of surprise. After all, the success of the mission will depend on it.

She hovers over her unsuspecting victim. She pauses. Then she flies in for the landing. Her prey fulfills all the important criteria: He is a heavy breather with an abundance of skin bacteria. The tiny villain, anxious to feed, pierces the prey's warm skin.

Suddenly, a large hand appears out of nowhere. There is a resounding slap.

"Gotcha," says her victim.

And the huntress never knew what hit her.

Cock-A-Doodle-Doo

"I want you to quit sitting on my fence and making a ruckus," says the pig one morning. "You're crowing is giving me a headache, and your droppings are making a mess."

"The farm is home to all its residents. I have every right to sit here," says the rooster with indignation.

"But you're ruining the best part of my day. Get out of here, you scoundrel."

"Make me."

The pig grunts and squeals. "Here comes the farmer with my lunch. We'll see what he has to say about the matter."

The rooster gets off the fence. "Okay, don't tie yourself up in knots, I'm leaving."

Philomena and Suma

The two orangutans are curious. But they aren't sure if they want another ape sharing their indoor exhibit. After all, they've had the run of the place for such a long time.

"What do you think about this new development?" says Philomena as she leans down beside Suma on the platform and ogles the newcomer, who is swinging among the tree branches.

"I'm not sure what to say," says Suma, gesturing as she stares at the new visitor with reddish-brown hair. "Maybe we should wait for her to come over to us."

The wait is a short one.

Dalinda

Dalinda shuffles on four stumpy legs from her lair to the water's edge. Bat-like wings attach to a muscular body that is a kaleidoscope of magnificent colours. Yellow eyes peer out at the world between long eyelashes. An elegant tail covered in scales sweeps the ground as she walks.

Suddenly a guttural cry escapes her throat. Her pupils dilate as he enters her peripheral vision. When she grins, several teeth poke out the sides of her mouth.

It is love at first sight.

Oscar

Where can he be? It's Christmas Eve, and it's getting late. The last time I saw him was two hours ago.

I open the front door and shiver. It's cold outside. "Oscar, where are you? Please come home!"

I head to the kitchen for a glass of warm milk. It usually helps me sleep. Not that I plan to get any sleep until I find my beloved companion.

Suddenly, I hear familiar barking. When I open the front door, I am nearly run over.

Oscar has finally come home.

Southbound

The first time I saw Mary was on Christmas Eve. We both waited for the train on the southbound subway platform. Her arms were laden with packages.

Although I tried not to stare, I couldn't help myself.

I didn't believe in love at first sight — not until that very moment.

She glanced over at me and smiled. "Hello," she said, laughter in her voice.

I was speechless — but not for long.

"Hello. Do you need my help?" I asked.

Years later, I still help Mary with her packages, although it doesn't have to be on Christmas Eve.

Santa's Got Mail

Dear Mr. Claus,

Regarding the full-time position of Elf on Santasgotnews.ca, please find attached a copy of my resume for your consideration.

One of the first graduates of an accredited toy-making college, I have 15 years of experience working in the toy shop of one of your largest competitors, a certificate in team leading, one in time management, and an Elf of the Year plaque.

I have been described as highly motivated and a team player.

If you would like to get in touch to discuss my application form and resume, you may reach me at reggie@snail.com.

Sincerely,

Reggie

Dear Reggie,

Thank you for your inquiry regarding the advertised position. But I'm afraid competition is fierce this year and your application is unsuccessful.

While your CV is extensive, I will make a few suggestions. I would like you to take a few courses in reindeer management, toy storage, stock control, and level 2 Chimney Geography.

Since courses are available in your local area in all of these fields, you won't have to venture too far.

Best wishes for a happy and prosperous New Year.

Yours sincerely,

Santa Claus

Rudolph

Mrs. Claus is exhausted. She needs a vacation. All she has to do now is convince her husband to go with her.

As she joins him in the workshop, she places a hand on his shoulder. "Lately, you've spent too much time in the workshop. Perhaps you need to take a break."

"Sweetheart, you know I can't leave the North Pole. I'm on a strict schedule. We don't want to disappoint the little children now, do we?"

"Kris, the elves can take charge this year. They're more than capable," says Mrs. Claus.

"Perhaps, but remember the last time we gave the elves free rein? They caused the reindeer nothing but grief. And Rudolph has never been the same."

Mrs. Claus

Outside the log cabin, snowflakes drift across a blue sky while reindeer forage for lichen.

Mrs. Claus glances sideways at her husband. "Sweetheart, take a holiday this Christmas. You deserve one."

Mr. Claus points to a box of children's letters that sits on his lap. "But who will deliver the gifts to the children?"

"I know the perfect person," she says with a smile. She giggles as she wraps her arms around her husband's portly form and kisses him on the cheek. "Although I may have to make a few alterations to your Santa suit."

Ho Ho Ho!

Darby hears Santa's voice as her hooves scrape crusted snow in search of dinner. She shifts her attention to a nearby barn where Santa holds court amidst a herd of reindeer.

She approaches the group with some trepidation. "Please take me with you tomorrow when you take out the sleigh," she pleads.

Santa studies Darby, his brow furrowed. "You're still in training."

"But I've almost finished the course. And I promise to work extra hard," says Darby.

Santa hesitates and then escorts his herd to a private area for a consultation.

His voice soon reverberates throughout the building. Snorts and grunts accompany his words. Before long, he returns to Darby's side with a smile on his face.

"Eight say yes. One will think about it."

On Christmas Eve, a joyful Darby joins Santa and his reindeer as they dash off into the night.

Boxing Day Specials

The lights flick on in the mall's department store.

A security officer waits, and then sternly warns the Boxing Day shoppers to back away from the doors.

"Please be patient," he says for the umpteenth time that morning when they try to push him out of the way. "There will be enough to go—"

But the doors suddenly fly open, the crowd surges ahead, and the officer disappears from view. He never does get to finish his sentence.

The Presents

Zoe stares in awe at the presents she has received this Christmas morning. Her parents have been more than generous.

But Zoe learns that some of her ten-year-old friends will not celebrate Christmas this year. Their fathers are unemployed.

"Mom, if it's okay with you, I'd like to give away some of my Christmas presents."

"Why, sweetheart?"

"It's cold this winter, and some of my friends could use an extra pair of socks or mitts. I have more than enough to go around."

Amy

Amy takes a deep breath and mounts her horse under a blazing sun. Sweat trickles down her neck and contributes to her discomfort.

"Goodness me," she mutters as she adjusts her cowboy hat and sits tall in the saddle.

Spirit stomps his feet, paws the ground, and appears out of sorts.

Amy bends down and rubs the side of his neck. "I mustn't forget the ears. They also deserve some attention."

Spirit neighs.

"And let's schedule the run for another day."

Spirit swings his tail.

Who says horses can't communicate!

Help

I check my watch. I rub my eyes. I still have no cell signal. I'm thirsty. I'm hungry. I can't remember the last time I ate. I'm living my worst nightmare. I wipe the sweat from my brow. I take a few deep breaths to fill my lungs and calm my nerves. I yell, "Help!" for the umpteenth time. I wonder if anyone can hear me. I detect muffled voices through the elevator door. It suddenly opens. I run for the nearest stairs.

Home Sweet Home

Alexia's eyes are closed while she relaxes on a lounge chair wearing her recently purchased bathing suit.

The sound of ocean waves resonates throughout the room and fills her with a sense of peace. Tropical island music permeates the air and transports her to another place.

She adjusts the wide-brimmed hat that shields her face from a shaft of light, which streams through a partially open window. She reaches for a glass of cold lemonade that sits on a nearby table.

Her husband appears in the entrance to the living room with a puzzled look on his face. "I'm sure there's a logical explanation for all this."

Alexia frowns. "Our trip to the islands is cancelled once again because of the coronavirus."

Daniel shakes his head. "I'll grab another chair from the basement and join you."

A New Adventure

He silences his alarm clock, suppresses a yawn, stumbles out of bed, and gets dressed. He checks the time, notices he's running late, seizes hold of his briefcase, and dashes out the door. He deposits his ticket at the subway station and waits on the platform. The train pulls in, the doors open, and he advances with the crowd. He exits the station, walks for several minutes, and then enters a building. A man greets him with a surprised look on his face and asks him why he's at work.

He suddenly remembers that he retired yesterday.

The Writer

After ten years of writing, day and night, Fiona has completed her first book. And the book-signing is today.

With books cradled in both arms and more squeezed into her backpack, she walks up to the manager of the bookstore.

"Are you buying all those books?"

"No, I'm your guest author today," says Fiona.

"Sorry, I completely forgot you were coming. Grab the empty table and chair," she says, pointing. "And best of luck."

Fiona sighs and then mutters an oath as she sits down beside the entrance to the restroom.

The Genie

Clifford is frustrated. His dreams are occurring far too frequently, and he wonders if it's an omen. One night he dreams a genie visits and hovers over his bed. Finding himself awake, he looks around the room, but no one is there. A whoosh of air lifts him off the bed and onto the floor. "I've got to stop rubbing oil into my scalp before I go to sleep," he mutters.

No Excuse

I come home after being away a week on business. Dirty dishes are piled in the sink. There must be a week's worth.

"You could have at least cleaned up after yourself," I say.

"You're a nag," he says with a hurt look on his face. "Besides mopping the floors, vacuuming the rugs, doing the laundry, cleaning out the cupboards, mowing the lawn, washing and taking the dog for his walk, I worked a twelve-hour shift in the emergency department."

"Okay," I say, "but that still doesn't explain the dirty dishes."

Brittany

Brittany sits in her black utility vehicle. Low-lying clouds offer a blanket of darkness, and tinted windows provide privacy.

The engine is off, so there is no heat.

She buries herself deeper into her spring jacket. She licks her dry lips but refuses to look at her thermos of coffee. She needs to focus.

Several hours later, her subject's car is still parked in the driveway. She needs to pee. It's the last time she agrees to work surveillance on Valentine's Day.

A Newer Model

Bob twists his ankle when he kicks the soccer ball into the net. He swears out loud and limps off the field.

Later that evening, his wife frowns. She tells him he shouldn't have been playing soccer in the first place.

"You're an old rooster," she says. "Sixty years old. You need to act your age."

Bob doesn't want to act his age. He doesn't feel old. He decides to ignore his wife's grumbling.

The next day he goes out and buys himself a red sports car.

This is followed up with a hair transplant and a gym membership.

But when he receives the estimate for a facelift, he decides it's time to curtail his spending.

The Note

Madison left me a note this morning. She attached it to the door of our refrigerator.

As always, it accompanies all her other notes.

There are so many, I'm losing count. This one is bright yellow. She might have forgotten that yellow is my least favourite colour.

You see, we seldom talk anymore.

I'm not sure when our communication ceased. It may have been after our children moved out of the house. Or it may have been the day I retired.

No, I think it was well before then.

She's busy all the time, or so she says. Perhaps she finds me boring. Perhaps it's my grey hair. Or maybe she has just stopped loving me.

We need to talk about it. I miss her. I'll leave her a note. A purple one. It's her favourite colour.

The Challenge

He lurks outside a bistro wearing a baseball cap, black sweatshirt, and sunglasses.

As Avery studies the window display across the street, she notices his reflection in the glass. The familiar figure rattles her senses. When he starts to pull up the sleeves of his sweatshirt, she wonders if he's hot under the blazing sun.

"It serves him right," she mutters.

After a few minutes, Avery continues to walk along the sidewalk. Shopping will have to wait.

Who knew buying her husband a birthday present would prove this difficult.

Beguiled

I rest on a bench, alone with my thoughts, the distractions from the world miles away, when a raven announces its presence. The distinctive croaking brings a smile to my face.

A sigh escapes my lips as I watch the ripples of water sparkle. And as I embrace the tranquility of my surroundings, it gently nourishes my soul.

I close my eyes and decide to remain a little longer.

An Oasis

Cherry trees with branches of pink blossoms sway in a gentle breeze. Warm rays from the morning sun amidst a clear blue sky caress our faces. Birds chirp and their songs fill the air as they fly from one branch to the next. Children race across the countryside and their laughter brings smiles to our faces.

Fear slips by the wayside. Peace and tranquility will prevail.

The Scent of Gardenia

William walked barefoot along the water's edge, basking in the warmth of the sun. Alone with only his memories to offer him companionship, his feet sank into familiar soft sand. Overhead, fluffy white clouds drifted across a bright-blue sky. In the distance, seagulls, with their frantic cries, performed acrobatic manoeuvres and floated on the wind. A gentle breeze infused with the scent of gardenia caressed his face and whispered his name.

He knew Stephanie was never far away.

Beloved

I watch my husband limp off the tennis court, bend over at the waist, and take a few deep breaths.

"You're no spring chicken!" I shout. "You need to look after yourself."

He says goodbye to his tennis partner, walks over, and kisses me on the cheek.

"You worry too much," he says and laughs.

I frame his face with my hands, kiss him on the mouth, and tell him that, after thirty years of marriage, I've earned the right.

"Don't ever change," he says as he grabs hold of my hand and gives me a smile.

George

I sit by the front door and wait. I wear a rumpled undershirt and sweatpants.

"That's all we could find that was clean, George," the nursing home staff tell me.

My family takes my clothes home to wash on the days they visit. But it has been several months since their last one.

I wonder if they're too busy looking after my grandchild. She turns four today, but we've never met. My son feels my old face, wrinkled skin, and hunched back may frighten her. So I keep quiet.

If I say anything, they may stop visiting altogether.

The Box

Several months after her death, Edward visited her side of the closet. There it was. The cardboard box sat on the top shelf just as his wife promised.

He recalled her final words: "Look inside, after I die."

His arthritic limbs protested as he climbed the two-step ladder, grabbed the box, and balanced it between his arms. After he descended, he placed it on a bedside table, lifted the lid, and reached inside.

His eyes stung with unshed tears as he opened the envelope and read the words.

"My dearest, I shall miss you."

The Summer of 2016

The day she visited the nursing home was one of the hottest on record. Inside, the air conditioning had started to malfunction, so she escorted her mother to an outdoor terrace. They sat on chairs adorned with vibrantly coloured cushions. And they welcomed soft breezes that delivered a delicious scent of blooms.

Timid eyes that still held a sparkle peeked out from under the brim of a large sun hat.

"Do I know you?" asked her mother for the umpteenth time that day.

Scott's Mother

Scott slowly walked into the visitor's lounge. He saw her frail form, ravaged by old age, sitting in a wheelchair. He knelt and reached for one of her pale, cold hands.

She cowered in fear, folded her arms across her chest, and tilted her head from side to side.

Eyes that were partially blinded by cataracts searched his face.

"Who are you?" she whispered.

"It's not important, Mother," said Scott, and he turned and walked away.

Until We Meet Again

Her father's words were muddled. He was incoherent. His once-bright eyes now fixed in a dull stare.

Clutching his cold, damp hand, she would be patient and find out what he was trying to tell her. Moving closer to the bed, she studied his ashen face, searched for a sign that he was still part of this life.

But eventually she faced the truth. Her father was dying.

Later, she whispered in his ear, "Until we meet again."

Just Like You

I remember the first time I saw you. I was eight years old, and you were ten. For me it was love at first sight.

I was the blond-haired girl with pigtails and braces. But I don't think you noticed me.

When I saw you again, I was nineteen. We spent a night together. You probably don't remember.

But how can I forget your clear blue eyes or the dimple on your chin?

I am now twenty-eight. I'm the woman who has a son that looks just like you.

Bright-Red Shoelaces

I am mesmerized by the shoe display in the shop's window. The red leather shoes with the four-inch heels beckon me. They'll look perfect with my little black dress.

But my bunions and calf muscles start to protest. I tell my feet to be patient as I leave the store an hour later. I'm wearing a new pair of black walking shoes with bright-red shoelaces. The red leather will have to wait.

The Treadmill

Ellie approaches her husband at the kitchen counter. "Let's go for a walk. It's beautiful outside."

"I need to prepare supper," says Jake and continues to peel the potatoes.

"But we're not eating for another hour," says Ellie and kisses him on the cheek.

"Why not use the treadmill," says Jake.

"At the moment, it serves another purpose," says Ellie.

"How so?"

"Remember how you promised to fix the clothes dryer two weeks ago," says Ellie.

"Yes. And it remains a work-in-progress," says Jake as he rinses the potatoes. "What does that have to do with the treadmill?"

Ellie gives her husband a playful poke in the ribs. "Well, after I drape the wet laundry over the frame, there's little room for me to exercise."

A Shave and a Haircut

"Jerry, I would like to see you today. I have something important to ask you," says his ninety-year-old mother into the phone's receiver.

Later that afternoon, Jerry enters his mother's bungalow.

"Okay, Mom. What's this all about?"

"Chuck has asked me to marry him. I would like you to walk me down the aisle."

Jerry bites his tongue as he ponders the couple's fifty-year age gap.

"I wonder what father would say."

"He'd probably tell you to get a shave and a haircut."

Oxyphenbutazone

She runs her tongue over her upper lip. She tastes the salty fluid and wrinkles her nose. Perspiration lines her brow.

She leans forward in her chair, elbows on the table, bloodshot eyes on the gameboard.

"I haven't got all day you know," he says.

"Please don't interrupt my concentration," she replies.

She arranges the tiles.

"Eureka!" she shouts. "Oxyphenbutazone. One thousand, four hundred and fifty-eight points. I keep the house. You get the tool shed."

Her husband places his hands over his face and groans.

Megaburger and French Fries

Heidi exits her gravel driveway and presses the accelerator with the tip of her shoe as soon as her car hits the pavement. She plans to keep the man in her sight. She gives her vehicle full throttle while she keeps her eyes peeled on the rear bumper of his car. She decelerates before she reaches the first curve in the road and accelerates on exit. She follows closely when he pulls into a fast-food drive and listens while he orders.

The megaburger, cola, and fries aren't allowed on her husband's diet plan. As far as she is concerned, all bets are now off.

Inked

Buffy is mesmerized by the images on the computer screen. Eye candy that spellbinds. What better way to celebrate her fiftieth birthday than with a tattoo?

She makes a call and arranges an appointment.

Weeks later, she inhales deeply, opens the door, and crosses the threshold into the studio. A tattoo artist escorts her to a work area. After they discuss designs and risks, Buffy climbs onto a tattoo bed. She shuts her eyes and prays this rite of passage is soon over. That evening, her sparkling blue eyes light up.

A small butterfly tattoo now adorns her left shoulder. Flashbacks of needles and discomfort all but fall by the wayside.

ASAP

"You have nice eyes. I could get lost in their depths," he says with a smirk.

Flee the coffee shop now, says her inner voice. *Make up an excuse. Say anything.*

She swallows. "Thank you for the compliment."

He leans in. "And your profile picture doesn't do you justice, which I'm sure you've been told."

"No, this is the first time." She grabs her purse and stands up. "Sorry, I need to let the dog out."

She makes a mental note. *Cancel the online dating service, ASAP.*

The Medieval Warrior

Riding through the dense forest, clad in armour, the medieval warrior hears rustling in the undergrowth. Movement in the trees makes her aware she's not alone.

Anticipating an altercation, Sloane brings her horse to a standstill and dismounts.

She draws her weapon from its sheath and holds it with a steady hand, ready to strike.

The approaching enemy is surprised by her prowess as she brandishes her sword. They soon learn not to underestimate this woman who carries a dangerous weapon.

Touché.

The Dental Assistant

Mark has a toothache. He's forgotten which day the pain started. The pandemic appears to have blurred all sense of time.

In the bathroom, he gargles with salt water.

"Please see the dentist," his wife says, as she places her hand on his shoulder.

He spits the bitter-tasting liquid into the sink and gags.

"I have some concerns about the latest dental assistant," he says.

"Why?" she asks.

"The robot is being difficult. It refuses to wear a shield and face mask," says Mark.

Jumping Josephat

Paul closed the front door behind him and headed for the living room.

The smell of paint fumes permeated the air.

"Honey!" he shouted. "I'm home."

"Hi, Paul," said his wife when she joined him, holding a paint brush in one hand.

"You painted the walls!"

"An idle paintbrush motivated me to give the room a fresh coat."

"But why such a bright colour?"

"You've always liked yellow," said Harper.

"On you, but not the wall," said Paul.

"You'll be glad to hear I also painted your man cave."

Paul raised his eyebrows. "Yellow?"

"Royal blue with white horizontal stripes," said Harper. "You'll love it."

"Jumping Josephat!" said Paul. "Perhaps you've had too much time on your hands during the pandemic."

Holy Moly

The sky was dark, and still no ski lodge in sight. And as snowflakes fell onto the windshield, the GPS failed.

Then her cell phone died.

Skylar shook her head in frustration, drove onto the shoulder of the road, and activated the emergency hazard lights. When the engine died, she hollered at the top of her lungs.

She squinted at a light in the distance. With renewed hope, she stepped out of the car and proceeded in the direction of the light.

An hour later, she stopped to catch her breath and leaned against a fence post. A sign affixed to a closed gate caught her attention: No Face Mask, No Entry.

She searched her purse, then remembered where she left her face mask.

Suffering succotash. It still dangled from her rear-view mirror.

Woof

Zoey follows the province's stay-at-home orders. No one is to leave their premises except for essential purposes.

Suddenly, she hears a strange noise. It comes from outside the house.

She opens the front door and sees a ventilated pet carrier standing on the doorstep. Printed on the side in bold letters are the words HANDLE WITH CARE.

What have we here? she wonders. "Woof."

She then remembers her visit to the local animal shelter.

She brings the carrier into her home, and Bear becomes acquainted with his new surroundings.

Izzy

I am elated when I find Izzy in the dumpster.

He prepares and serves me yummy meals. He loads and empties the dishwasher. He takes out the garbage, mops the floors, cleans the toilet and the sinks. He vacuums the living room. He washes, irons, and folds my clothes. He removes expired food from the refrigerator. He sorts the mail and takes phone messages. He changes light bulbs. He maintains the car. He mows, trims, and waters the lawn whether it needs it or not. And he is my personal security guard.

He played with the cat until the cat disappeared. He walked the dog until the dog ran away.

Now my robot wants a raise. What's a girl to do?

The Perfect Gift

Kate fell in love as soon as they met, and he accompanied her home that very same day.

His big, soulful eyes and sweet manner sent her lonely heart racing. He would be her perfect Valentine's Day gift, forever and always.

But as he curled up in her lap later that evening, she came to a final decision. Potty training would be non-negotiable.

The Game

He scrutinizes the seven tiles on his rack. He forms a word and places it on the board. He then turns to his wife.

She compresses her lips and leans forward. Her elbows rest on the kitchen table. The palm of one hand cradles her chin while her eyes dart between her tiles and the gameboard.

Thirty minutes later, he runs his fingers through his unruly hair and fidgets on his chair. "Hurry up, sweetheart, I haven't got all day."

"Quiet, please. I need to concentrate," she says, squeezes his knee, and then places all her tiles.

Soon after, she waves the score sheet in the air and yells, "I win!"

He breathes a sigh of relief and runs to the bathroom.

The Home Improvement Course

Noah shakes the Christmas present and holds it up to his ear. He removes the colourful wrapping, lifts off the lid, and studies the contents. Noah is rendered speechless.

His wife looks at him expectantly. "So, what do you think?"

"Thank you, sweetheart. You're way too generous," he says. Noah removes a selection of electrical tools and accessories from the box and places them on the floor.

"You can finally start that home improvement course you've been talking about for the last two years," she says, unable to disguise her delight.

Sticky Pecan Pie

Michelle leans against a tree, removes her gloves, and checks her watch. It's 9:00 a.m.

It's chilly this fall morning. She's cold, her back is sore, and she has now waited for over an hour.

She walks over and joins the group on the sidewalk.

A door opens, and a man exits the bakeshop.

He approaches and addresses the crowd. "Sorry everyone, we've sold out of the sticky pecan pie. Please come back tomorrow."

Half a Kilogram

She reduced her calorie intake. She ingested foods high in soluble and insoluble fibre. She doubled her servings of leafy green vegetables. She reduced her consumption of sugary drinks. She ate a variety of nuts and seeds. She increased her fluid intake. Every day, she worked out for thirty minutes in the gym, climbed a flight of stairs, and took the dog for a walk.

After fourteen days and losing only half a kilogram, she asked herself, *What gives?*

And she came to a foregone conclusion: She eats her food too fast.

Crispy Fish and Chips

Claire stares at her husband's dinner plate. His steamed vegetables and baked fish remain untouched.

"Tonight's fish is tasty. I've added extra herbs," says Claire and takes another mouthful of food.

"I'm not hungry. Every week I gain another pound," says Kevin and shakes his head in frustration. "I don't understand it."

"You can always call off the bet," says Claire.

"No way!" says Kevin. "I need to clear my head. I'm going for a drive." He gets up and walks out the door.

On impulse, Claire grabs her car keys and follows him at a discreet distance.

"One order of crispy fish and chips, please," says Kevin into the fast-food microphone.

As soon as he drives off, Claire places her order. And she asks for an extra helping of coleslaw on the side.

New Year's Resolution

Blood flows with great force through his arteries while the muscles in his legs contract painfully. He hears blood pounding in his ears as his arms pump vigorously by his side.

The pores of his body secrete sweat that drips from his forehead and trickles down his neck. After he clenches his fist, he grits his teeth and then collapses in a state of exhaustion onto the road.

Obituary: Sean was able to complete a New Year's Resolution — to run a long-distance race. May he now rest in peace.

Worth the Wait

She takes a deep breath, squeezes into a pair of skinny jeans, and tops it off with a chunky white sweater. She purses rouge-stained lips and practises a sultry pout in the hall mirror. She tucks her unruly red curls beneath a long black wig. Then she pulls on a pair of knee-high boots to give the illusion of longer legs but apologizes to her bunions.

One last time, she glances at her reflection, gives a conspiratorial wink, and calls a cab.

After she walks into the restaurant, she spots him at a table.

"Happy birthday, sweetheart." She leans down and kisses her forty-year-old husband on the cheek. "Sorry I'm late."

He smiles. "Some things are worth the wait."

The Proposal

Cora removes the last item from the package and sets it on the shelf. After she shuts the closet door, she breathes a sigh of relief. Soon she will have to find other places to store her precious belongings.

Logan appears in the doorway of the spare room. He stumbles over a roll of toilet paper and mutters a curse.

Startled, Cora turns and faces her husband. "I just put away the rest of the holiday decorations."

Logan gives her a questioning look. "I thought you did that weeks ago."

"I forgot a few ornaments," says Cora as she links arms with her husband. "Come on. I'll make us lunch."

Her proposal to stockpile toilet paper in the event of a global shortage may not pass muster with her husband.

Gobsmacked

You open your door and find business-sized envelopes on the front porch.

Your phone rings just as you toss them on the kitchen table.

When you answer, an automated messaging system causes your heart to rapidly beat in your chest. Your hands shake.

Flustered, the phone slips from your grasp.

Weeks later, more envelopes cover the porch, and your voicemail is inundated with messages to upgrade your plan.

Gobsmacked, you wonder when you became so popular.

You take a deep breath, scream, and then send a cease and desist letter to your cell phone provider.

A Whirligig

Wind-driven ice pellets batter the front windshield as Maggie inches down the highway.

Her grip on the steering wheel tightens. She squints as she leans forward in the driver's seat.

Headlights flash in her rear-view mirror. Her vehicle shakes as a transport truck passes by.

Soon after, something strikes her windshield and lodges in the dashboard. Then her vehicle hits a patch of black ice, spins like a whirligig, and plummets into a ditch along the highway.

She lets out a blood-curdling scream and prays for a miracle.

"Miss, are you okay?"

She wonders if the voice is real.

The door on the driver's side opens.

Maggie is at a loss for words, the first time in her life.

Unfinished Business

Tom visits his favourite Asian takeout. After dinner, he opens the refrigerator and stares at the shelves filled with paper containers. He sighs and shakes his head. He removes a container and replaces it with his unfinished meal.

"Forget takeout. Time for some cooking lessons," he mutters.

Lilith and the Vampires

One Halloween, Lilith dipped her apples in the hot caramel, and then set them down to dry. She untied her apron, laid it on the counter, and happened to look out the window.

Trick-or-treaters, their bodies enveloped in long black shrouds, were kneeling in her pumpkin patch, their faces buried in some of the garden's biggest shells.

But since the light was fading, Lilith wondered if her eyes were deceiving her.

"Oh my goodness," she said, blinked a few times, and then pressed her nose up against the windowpane. But the trespassers were still there, and they reminded her of well-dressed vampires.

Lilith enjoyed Halloween. But anyone who dressed up in a vampire costume spooked her. She wondered if her parents' obsession with horror films, mythological beings, and cemeteries during her youth had something to do with it. And she blamed them for the nightmares every few months.

Soon after they were married, Lilith's husband received an inheritance. "I'm getting tired of the city," he said one day. "I'd like to move to the countryside."

Lilith enjoyed living in the city, and she was not in a hurry to move. "Let me think about it, Chief," she said.

But Walter continued to check houses for sale in the local newspaper.

"There's a bungalow for sale, but it's across from a cemetery," he said.

"I'm not sure I want to live that close to a cemetery," said Lilith. "Although it could someday save us transportation costs."

"Listen, Lilith," said Walter, "it would be nice and peaceful in the country, and we wouldn't have to put up with visits from trick-or-treaters. There's no way parents would want to venture far away from home on Halloween."

So Walter eventually convinced Lilith that moving was the right decision.

Walter was hard of hearing, so Lilith yelled his name at the top of her voice while she fixated on the scene outside. "Walter, come here!"

"What do you want? You know I hate being interrupted during the evening news," he shouted from the next room.

"Well, isn't that just too bad, because there are a couple of trespassers dressed in shrouds sampling our pumpkins," she said. "Get out there and tell them to get off the property."

But Lilith had no way of knowing her trespassers were a couple of supernatural beings who had recently taken up residence in nearby Sleepy Oaks Cemetery. Several days of no food, boredom, and receiving the silent treatment from the occupants motivated the beings to wander off the grounds. And in their search for sustenance, they happened upon Lilith's garden. Their eyes lit up like beacons as they gazed upon the bright-orange fruit.

"Yuck, this tastes awful," hissed Constantine minutes later as he spit out a mouthful of pulp. "This tastes nothing like blood. There has to be something to eat around here."

"You're telling me. But this isn't it," said Elena throwing down her pumpkin and staring at it in disgust.

She looked up at the house, wiped her mouth with the back of her hand, and glanced over at her boyfriend with a mischievous grin. "Let's go."

Lilith was immersed in the events unfolding in the pumpkin patch. She continued to watch in amazement as her trespassers nodded their heads. With shrouds billowing, they started to make their way toward the bungalow.

Before Lilith had a chance to lock the back door, it opened. Suddenly she felt very cold.

"Those pumpkins just aren't cutting it. There has to be something else to eat or drink around here," said Elena.

Lilith froze.

"Walter, get over here now," said Lilith, her voice barely more than a whisper.

The intruders' dark eyes sparkled. They grinned, licked their lips, and approached Lilith with joyful anticipation.

Frightened, Lilith screamed and reached for the candy apples. But she had a feeling her guests were interested in more than Halloween treats.

Happy Halloween

Hector opens the door and steps onto the porch. Picking up the morning paper, he takes a swat at paper bat mobiles that are attached to the ceiling. The chilly air is all but forgotten after he sees Halloween symbols scattered around the yard.

Jack-o'-lanterns with a variety of facial expressions line the driveway. Skeletons with movable joints swing in the wind as they hang off tree branches. A nursery of raccoons climbs into a witch's cauldron that stands in the middle of the lawn.

Hector mutters and shakes his head. It appears his wife has been busy.

His wife joins him and places an arm around his waist. "What do you think?"

He glances at her Wonder Woman costume and laughs. "Halloween is still weeks away!"

Joyful Anticipation

A few hours after sunset, Alessandro headed for the gates at the cemetery exit. Rain pounded his cloaked back while howling winds assaulted his ear drums. The sound reminded him of the anguished cries of his ancestors who might have lost their way. As his fingers probed his cloak pockets for additional warmth, he heard shrieks of laughter that seemed to be coming from somewhere nearby. He stopped for a moment, looked around, saw no one, so continued on his way. After all, he needed to get out of this wretched place, and the sooner, the better.

He was hungry, though strapped for cash. He was thirsty, and the coffin he had inhabited for the last several days offered little in the way of creature comforts. Damp and musty, it sent his olfactory receptors and his pulse into a frenzy. It reminded him too much of home.

He lifted his hood over a mane of unruly black hair and growled when another gust of wind unleashed its fury and nearly pushed him over.

"Cripes," he muttered through his long, pointed teeth as he staggered a short distance.

A group of revellers in Halloween costumes surprised him at the gate.

"Trick or treat!" the exuberant adults shouted in unison. And after they complimented him on his costume, they held out a bag of goods and offered him a treat.

"Thank you for sharing. I also have a special treat for you tonight," said Alessandro with a toothy grin and licked his lips. His black eyes adopted a steely glint as he admired the exposed necks of his new-found friends.

He would feast tonight.

A Head Start

Celeste is elated. Fall is her favourite time of year.

She gazes upon a darkened sky with expressive black eyes. She sports a look of gleeful anticipation while her tongue teases a jewelled fang.

Gusty winds release unbridled fury while revellers in costumes plod along a well-trodden path near her grave.

Celeste licks her lips. "Hello," she says, perched atop her headstone and wrapped in a bright-red cape. "But aren't you a little early for Halloween?"

The Thingamabob

Cliff looks out the kitchen window of his farmhouse. A round object that resembles a flying saucer sits on his plowed field.

"Millie, is there anything on the morning news about unusual sightings in this area?"

His wife joins him at the window. "Why, Cliff?"

"Well, an object with a saucer-shaped body has come to rest on our property."

"Oh, that silly thing," replies Millie. "The aliens came into our house as soon as they landed."

Cliff looks at Millie with a wary expression. "I told you not to talk to strangers."

"I really had no choice. They like to get up close and personal."

"So, what do they want?

"You can ask them yourself. They're standing right behind you."

A Reasonable Explanation

In the morning, he stared at his wife as she entered the kitchen. He held a set of car keys in his hand.

She told him to chill out, there was a reasonable explanation for her absence last night, and he shouldn't jump to conclusions.

"You shouldn't drive while you're angry. Please let me explain," she pleaded.

"Lately, I've listened to all your explanations," he said. He turned around and walked away.

"Come back, and we'll talk about it!" she yelled at his retreating back.

His funeral was held the following week, so she never did get a chance to explain.

Resus

Rachel shivers on the cold stretcher. Though emotionally drained, she thinks about the last exchange with her husband. But some details are a blur. She cringes at the sound of voices outside the partially open door.

"If your wife's heart stops again, do you want us to resuscitate?"

"We discussed it last evening. She said no."

Then she remembers the argument she lost.

Heartbeat

Carter's heart pounds in his chest, and he finds it difficult to breathe.

His wife stares at him across the breakfast table and frowns. "I'll call an ambulance." And she takes out her cell phone.

"It's only indigestion. It'll go away," says Carter.

Naomi ignores her husband and calls an ambulance.

The ambulance soon arrives and takes him to the emergency department of a local hospital.

"Mr. Smith," someone says while he lies on a stretcher, "can you hear me?"

But the voice fades and everything goes dark.

Carter takes his final breath as he floats higher and higher. As he looks down at his body, Carter notices that his hospital gown has been removed and his chest exposed.

"Stop!" he shouts. "Please, leave me alone."

But no one is listening. They are too busy pounding on his chest.

Minutes pass and then hours before he finally awakens and feels his wife's kiss on his cheek.

If Only

You wrinkle your nose at medicinal smells that creep under your mask and tease your olfactory senses.

You adopt a wide stance in anticipation of a sneeze.

You reflect on happier times while you stand behind a glass partition that separates you from your husband of twenty years.

It is far too long since your last visit. But the matter is out of your hands. You have no say during this pandemic.

You watch him lie motionless under white hospital sheets, his eyes closed.

Your eyes burn with unshed tears as you see him take shallow breaths.

You clench your fist, lean forward, and strike the cold tempered glass.

You grimace in pain, your eyes water, but the scream dies on your lips.

You feel the artery in your neck pulsate at an alarming rate. The discomfort is a reminder that you are very much alive.

Between partially open window drapes, sunlight streams into the hospital room and encircles the head of your loved one like a golden halo.

His hair shimmers, and it reminds you of the wheat fields back home.

You long to tear off your mask and run to his bedside. You long to pull him close, kiss his cheek one last time, and whisper in his ear, "I love you."

Instead, you bow your head, say a prayer, and wish the pandemic were nothing more than a thing of the past.

You feel a hand on your shoulder. You feel surprisingly calm and ask, "Who is there?"

There is no answer, but you know you are no longer alone.

Frailty of Life

I stand outside her hospital room as disinfectant permeates the air. I wrinkle my nose in distaste at the medicinal smell. My sixth sense tells me that today is important: My mother may have something to tell me, and I'll need to listen closely.

I stand by her bed and watch her take shallow breaths. Beams of morning light filter through window blinds and bounce off wisps of white hair. A white sheet hints at the fragile form beneath.

It has been only a few weeks since my last visit, but I notice how she has aged during my absence. The sheer futility of the situation tugs at my heartstrings, and for a moment it renders me alone and helpless. But I need to accept the inevitable: I need to start letting go.

Her eyelids flutter open, and she looks up at me with a puzzled expression. She grips the side rails. Her knuckles turn white. Her fear is palpable. So I smile, lean over, and press my cheek against hers.

"Hello, mother," I whisper in her ear.

She begins to shiver. I take a wool shawl out of her bedside drawer and wrap it around her shoulders.

After I kiss her on the forehead, I look her in the eye and search for recognition.

"Do I know you?" she asks.

My eyes fill with tears. "Yes," I say, and I turn my head.

One More Day

He just turned fifty. A few grey hairs are creeping toward his temple. There are too many candles to blow out. And he has too little energy.

He sits in his favourite chair but is in no mood to celebrate. His heart beats rapidly. He feels trepidation as he tries to catch a breath.

His wife flashes him a look of concern, but immediately, it disappears.

She strokes his shoulder, kisses his cheek, and whispers in his ear, "I love you."

He tells her his pain is unimportant, there's no reason to be alarmed, it's probably indigestion, and, like always, will go away.

His wife calls an ambulance. The siren screams a warning as the ambulance races through busy city streets.

The doors make a whooshing noise as they open and close.

People call his name, tap his shoulder, and ask if he can hear them.

He prays for the first time in his life. He asks for another minute, another hour, another day.

His wife kisses him on the cheek when he later opens his eyes. "Happy Birthday, sweetheart."

Patience

He watches him through a panel of glass. He loves it when he smiles. He longs to remove his mask and give his father a hug. But the nursing home will not allow it.

Tomorrow is another day, he tells himself. Be patient.

He has all the time in the world for his father.

A Fresh Start

She opens the window and leans out. She claps her hands as people sing and dance in the streets below.

Snowflakes drift from the night sky, touch flushed cheeks, and then disappear.

She feels at peace and in good health.

She longs to make a fresh start.

Cut and Tie

Bill, a father of eight, is transferred on a stretcher to the operating room.

His wife paces the waiting room.

"What's taking them so long?" she asks the receptionist an hour later.

Suddenly there's an overhead announcement. "Code yellow. All staff conduct a search of your immediate area for a missing patient. Please call 9111 to receive the description."

Olivia is startled when her husband's urologist taps her on the shoulder. There's a minor delay. "Once I've located your husband, I'll be able to continue with the procedure," he whispers. "He's being skittish."

Later that evening, a frustrated Olivia kisses her sleeping husband on his cheek. Her health is her first priority.

She lifts the bed sheet off her husband and positions the scalpel — then pauses.

Tomorrow they'll have a serious talk about other options.

Final Warning

Molly's eyes follow the nurse as she enters the postpartum room. Perspiration soaks Molly's flimsy blue gown. She fights the urge to close her sleep-deprived eyes.

She remembers her husband's last words before he collapsed on the delivery-room floor. "I am going to be sick."

The nurse approaches her bed, smiles, and places a hand on Molly's shoulder. "The doctor says your husband will be just fine."

Molly nibbles her lower lip. She breathes a sigh of relief. But this is the last time she will invite Nate into the delivery room.

Blood Splatter

Blood spurted out of his severed artery, shot against the wall, and splattered to form its own unique pattern.

"You know I hate guns in the house," said his wife earlier that day.

"It's for your own protection," said her husband while he cleaned his pistol. "There has been a rash of burglaries in the neighbourhood. But let's have this discussion some other time. I'm tired and I need to lie down."

Later that day, she studied the wall. And she wondered what colour she would paint it this time.

Scattered

His undivided attention smothered her. There were the breakfast trays that appeared on her lap each morning. Scribbled love notes shoved under tear-stained pillows. There were kisses planted on turned cheeks. There were bruises hidden under long-sleeved sweaters. And heart-shaped boxes of chocolates on Valentine's Day. Promises made but never kept. Birthday presents no longer appreciated. Fractured bones. A heart unable to mend.

And ashes scattered from a fire ignited long ago.

A Bad Dream

She feels ambivalent as she pauses outside the investigator's office and clutches a handful of photos. She shakes her head in anger and shoves them into an envelope.

She climbs into the driver's seat of her vehicle and exits the parking lot. Minutes later, she pulls onto a freeway.

A squeal of tires assaults her eardrums. The smell of burning rubber overloads her senses. The scrape of metal sends off a shower of sparks. Then the ominous tones of wailing sirens fill the countryside.

A white hospital sheet covers Rachel's unconscious body. Strands of wavy brown hair matted in blood peek from under a stained dressing wrapped around her skull. Long eyelashes rest on pale cheeks.

The smell of antiseptic lingers. Voices of hospital staff whisper through a partially open door and blend with the rhythm of a mechanical ventilator.

Suddenly, the ventilator is interrupted by a spontaneous breath.

But the bedside nurse remains calm. She adjusts the rate of red blood cells flowing into Rachel's veins.

A bedside monitor displays her heart rate at one hundred and forty beats per minute — until her blood pressure plummets to numbers that require immediate attention.

Months later, Rachel, drenched with perspiration, lets out a blood-curdling scream.

Travis kisses his wife's cheek and pulls her close. "Wake up, sweetheart," he says. "You must have had another bad dream."

The Policy

Chloe sits by the bedside and stares at her husband. Outside the hospital window, snowflakes fall from a grey sky.

Desmond opens his eyes and tries to sit up but grimaces in pain.

"Try not to move," says Chloe in a stern voice as she shifts her hips to get more comfortable.

Desmond's head throbs as he recalls the previous evening, the gun in his wife's hand, the bullet that grazed his shoulder.

And he realizes that increasing the coverage of his life insurance policy on her birthday was one big mistake.

The Summons

She discreetly watches the man from a corner of the subway platform. From the picture in her photo gallery, there is no doubt. He's the one.

After the train enters the station, she follows him through the automatic doors and sits in the seat beside him.

"You look familiar," she says.

He glances her way with an appreciative look. "I usually don't talk to strangers, but today I may make an exception." He extends his hand. "I'm Lee Spencer, by the way."

She removes an envelope from her tote bag and hands it to him. It's a summons to appear in court.

He makes a mental note to mind his own business next time.

Please Hold

1:00 p.m.

Lottie's flash fiction story is nearly complete. But she loses her internet connection.

"This can't be happening," she says while staring at her computer screen, willing it to connect. "I still need access to an online database."

Lottie calls her company's service line.

Lottie: "Hello, I would like to speak with—"

Robot: "I'm sorry, our agents are currently busy helping other callers, but your call is important to us. Please hold. We will be with you shortly."

Lottie: "Yes, but—"

Music starts to blare from her phone's speakers.

1:30 p.m.

Robot: "Thank you for waiting. We will be with you shortly. Have you checked our website? It may be able to provide you with a possible answer."

Lottie: "You've got to be kidding."

2:00 p.m.

Robot: "Thank you for continuing to hold."

Lottie now has a headache and rubs her forehead. She runs into the kitchen, grabs a bottle of water, holds it against her forehead, and returns to her computer screen. Still no connection.

3:00 p.m.

> *Robot:* "Your call is important to us. Please continue to hold."

Lottie shakes her head in frustration. She yearns for a live voice.

> *Robot:* "Please try again tomorrow. We are open for business at eight o'clock a.m. Goodbye."

Lottie swears and goes in search of a dictionary.

The Shelter

A chill is in the night air as shoppers avoid eye contact and hurry over snow-covered sidewalks.

Pain sears his muscles and joints as he pushes a metal cart filled with all his worldly possessions. An ill-fitting coat covers his gaunt frame. A toque hides the gash on his forehead. A cardboard shelter behind a coffee shop awaits his arrival minutes later.

He grabs the sandwich and the cup of soup that sit by the entrance. And he crawls inside, away from prying eyes.

Déjà Vu

I enter the waiting room and feel a sense of déjà vu. I shiver, and my heart beats rapidly. I take a few deep breaths. I find it always calms my jittery nerves.

I sit down in a chair and bury my face behind a magazine. A pungent odour invades my personal space and causes me to sneeze.

"Gesundheit," says someone behind an acrylic shield.

I try to ignore a high-pitched sound from somewhere nearby. It causes me to cringe and bite my lip. As I creep toward the exit, I hear a shout.

"Come back here, Susan! The dentist will see you now."

I mutter to myself, turn around, and reluctantly follow the dental assistant. I guess I can always use another toothbrush.

Claustrophobia

"I'm Emma. I have an appointment at nine-thirty."

"I'm Luke, one of the dental hygienists. Before you enter the office, I need to scan your forehead with this thermometer."

"Go ahead."

"You have no temperature. Good. Please sanitize your hands from the dispenser on the wall, follow me, and walk two metres behind."

"Where's Annie?"

"We've lost a number of hygienists since the start of the pandemic."

"Died?"

"No idea. The examining room is on the right. Shove aside the plastic panel that hangs in the doorway and sit on the chair. I'll be in shortly."

Emma's heart beats rapidly. She feels a pain in her chest and runs out of the dental office. "Come back!" a voice yells.

But she's not coming back.

A Sixth Sense

He needs to act quickly. After all, curious eyes could be on him at this very moment. He advances up the walkway holding a paper bag. He places the bag by his feet, removes a set of house keys from his coat pocket, and quickly unlocks the door.

A flash of dark fur followed by an excited bark descends upon him and knocks him off his feet. But nothing ever escapes that dog of his. He can smell his treats a mile away.

Lickety-Split

Eagerly, she leans forward on her chair. Her eyes are wide in anticipation as she studies the television screen. With no room on the shelf for more kitchen appliances, the deal of the day still piques her interest.

"So what are you watching?" asks her husband after he enters the living room.

She points to the screen then jots down some information. "A shopping channel's state-of-the-art pressure cooker."

He walks over and squeezes her shoulder. "I thought you bought one last month?"

She smiles and looks at him. "Yes, but this cooker lets me make a large batch of hard-boiled eggs, lickety-split. And they'll be easy to peel."

He rolls his eyes as he reflects on his wife's backyard chickens.

The hens and their nightly cackling wreak havoc on his sleep.

Farm Fresh Eggs

It's a beautiful spring morning, and Jenny decides to support the local farmers.

"Nothing tastes better than fresh farm eggs," she says as she sets off for the countryside.

"Oh, fiddlesticks!" she shouts hours later as the car stalls one more time. Her fault for driving on half a tank of gas.

She locks her car door and sets off.

An hour later, wiping sweat from her brow, she reads a sign on a fence post.

NO EGGS TODAY. THE HEN IS ON STRIKE.

NO FUEL. THE FARM'S TANK IS EMPTY.

The Elimination

She wiggles into a pair of tight jeans that accentuate her curvy figure. She purses her rouge-stained lips and practises a playful pout in front of the mirror. She conceals her unruly red curls beneath a black wig. She slips into a pair of high-heel boots to give the illusion of longer legs. She drops a fully loaded handgun into her tote bag before she heads for the door. She takes a final look in the mirror and gives herself a mischievous wink. Her competition at the singles mixer will never know what hit them.

A Bad Idea

The man recognizes the pistol as a Glock. And judging from her grim expression and fighting stance, this is not a social call.

"Where is she?" demands the visitor, as she advances.

The victim keeps his eyes focused on her steady hand and slowly backs up.

"I don't know who you're talking about," he responds, as he clenches his fists, and beads of moisture settle in frown lines.

Maybe giving his mistress the pistol as a Christmas gift was a bad idea.

Andy

Good morning. I have several perfectly reasonable requests to make before we start the day. I know, I know. I am a cell phone. How is that even possible? Okay, just humour me.

Request #1: I see that you placed a piece of cinnamon roll in your mouth. Now you are licking your fingers. You can touch me, only after washing your hands, since smudges and I do not see eye to eye. By the way, another piece of bread just fell out of your mouth and has landed on me. Oh, my goodness. Next time, you might want to chew with your mouth closed.

Request #2: Every once in a while, please clean my screen. No, not with the dirty towel the dog likes to drag across the living room floor. For your information, I respond best to a gentle wipe from a microfibre cloth. It is far more effective.

Request #3: We are on our way to the bathroom again, are we? If memory serves me right, we were just in there. It may have something to do with that cinnamon bun you ate. Try gluten-free next time. I am sure your intestinal tract will thank you. Or enter the bathroom without me. Instead, take a magazine or two. You have my permission. Anyway, I need my alone time.

Request #4: Please keep me off the rim of the bathtub. A previous incident serves as a reminder. You sat me on the rim. I slipped and landed on the bottom. It was quite the ride, and I still experience blackouts.

Request #5: Okay, if you must hold me while you do your business, please make it snappy. I have plans for the day.

Request #6: I am not waterproof, so try not to drop me in the toilet bowl. That one time was more than enough.

Request #7: Please wash your hands. I never know where they've been.

Bug-Eyed

Thank you for everything you do.

The water conditioner that prevents toxic buildup. The filter that generates water movement and supplies different types of filtration. The heater to keep me warm and comfortable. An air pump to supply me with oxygen. The lights that illuminate and enhance my pretty colours. The plants and decorative rocks that keep me company and give me a cozy atmosphere. And thank you for providing me with a healthy diet.

But the verdict is still out on Mr. Whiskers.

The Agent

She leans forward in her chair. She will attempt to extrapolate more information, though the agent's dossier is thorough.

Igor knows he's under suspicion. It's obvious by the look on her face after they escort him into the commander's office. His wife is respected for her brilliant mind and keen perception, and he wonders how long she has known.

He has taken every precaution but knew it would just be a matter of time before she was onto him.

He must have been talking in his sleep again.

Balloons

Winnie turns on the television and listens to the news. Today they're talking about different activities seniors can participate in to stay happy and healthy.

She turns off the set and glances toward her husband, who sits at the end of the sofa.

"We need to come up with an outdoor activity that gets us off the couch and into the fresh air," says Archibald.

"Follow me," says Winnie. She picks up several water balloons. She steps onto the balcony and lets the balloons drop on the plants below.

"I knew these balloons would come in handy, someday," she says.

The Dog Stays

Due to our compatibility and communication issues, and after giving it careful consideration, I am terminating our relationship.

Effective immediately, I am resigning as your nurse, housekeeper, personal trainer, masseuse, psychiatrist, event planner, personal secretary, pedicurist, and ear hair trimmer.

Please do not text or leave messages on my phone.

Christmas gifts (which include a skillet, food processor, beach towel, stuffed teddy bear, bracelet with fake pearls, packaged underwear in lime green, extra-large Christmas sweater, elf socks, and bamboo back scratcher) will be donated to a good home.

But the dog stays.